Why?

or, How a Peasant Got Into the Land of Anarchy

Abba and Wolf Gordin

TRANSLATED AND INTRODUCED BY
JESSE S. COHN AND EUGENE KUCHINOV

Why? or, How a Peasant Got Into the Land of Anarchy
By Abba and Wolf Gordin
This edition © 2023 AK Press (Chico / Edinburgh)
Introduction & translation © 2023 Jesse S. Cohn and Eugene Kuchinov

ISBN: 978-1-84935-502-5
E-ISBN: 978-1-84935-503-2
Library of Congress Control Number: 2022948754

AK Press
370 Ryan Ave. #100
Chico, CA 95973
www.akpress.org
akpress@akpress.org

AK Press
33 Tower St.
Edinburgh EH6 7BN
Scotland
www.akuk.com
akuk@akpress.org

The above addresses would be delighted to provide you with the
latest AK Press distribution catalog, which features books, pamphlets,
zines, and stylish apparel published and/or distributed by AK Press.
Alternatively, visit our websites for the complete catalog, latest news,
and secure ordering.

Cover design and interior illustrations by Y_Y. You can find their work
at @doublewhy_y.

Printed in the USA on acid-free paper

Contents

INTRODUCTION

by Jesse Cohn and Eugene Kuchinov

Fools and Weaklings

Subject: Khaidar, age twenty-five, collective
worker, barely literate.

What has changed in you yourself of late?
"Before I was a farmhand, I worked for a boss and
didn't dare talk back to him; he did with me as he
pleased. Now I know what my rights are ..."

What sort of qualities do you think an intelligent man has?
"If a man has studied since childhood and learns
to write, we say that he has become an intelligent
man. But if he doesn't learn, but just rides his
donkey and sings songs, and knows nothing about
where people come from, we say that he's a fool."
　　　　—ALEXANDER LURIA, *Cognitive Development*[1]

---

1. Alexander Luria, *Cognitive Development: Its Cultural and
Social Foundations*, trans. Martin Lopez-Morillas and Lynn

We are ashamed
to be smart
among fools.
              —ABBA L. GORDIN AND WOLF L. GORDIN,
                              Daloy Anarkhiyu![2]

ACCORDING TO BORIS YELENSKY'S memoir of the
Russian Revolution, the book you now hold in your
hands, originally published in 1918 by the Moscow
Federation of Anarchist Groups as number sixteen in
their "Biblioteka Anarkhista" series, was "the one pamphlet that Abba Gordin ever wrote in his life that had real
potential as propaganda."[3] As proof, Yelensky tells the
following story: on his travels across Ukraine, Yelensky
tried to befriend Alexei, a young worker from the country who was the attendant assigned to his railway coach.
In those early days of the Revolution, Alexei looked with
suspicion on Yelensky's assurances that the two of them

Solotaroff, ed. Michael Cole (Cambridge, MA: Harvard University Press, 1976), 157–58.

2. Abba L. Gordin and Wolf L. Gordin, *Daloy Anarkhiyu!*
[Down with anarchy!] (Petrograd, 1917), 750.

3. Leonid Heller asserts that it was the first literary utopia written after the February Revolution, that it was written
in Petrograd in 1917, even before the October Revolution (in
Leonid Heller, "Voyage au pays de l'anarchie: Un itinéraire:
L'utopie," *Cahiers du Monde russe* 37, no. 3 (July–September 1996):
258). As will be seen, there are grounds for doubting both that it
was written before October and that it was written in Petrograd.
Most likely the text of *Why?* was completed in the autumn of
1917 and published at the end of 1917 (or even early 1918).

might eat a meal and drink tea together; was this a trick? But it was this book that broke the spell. Alexei picked up a copy that had been left out in the open and continued reading it whenever his passengers were not present. He soon had urgent questions: "What is anarchism? Where is this kingdom [*sic*] found?" The young man then sought additional copies of *Why?* to circulate in his village. "Our movement had found an unlooked-for sympathizer!" Yelensky concludes.[4]

Was this Alexei just a credulous young man, apt to believe whatever he read? On the contrary, his wariness was manifest. "Is what is written in the pamphlet merely a fantasy?" he demanded to know. Yelensky's reply was just as cautious: "I answered him that the pamphlet was written in the form of a fantastical story but that this fantasy could become a fact in the real life of the whole world, one where there will be no hunger and no want, and all people shall be equal citizens [*gleykhe birger*]."[5] That this won over someone who had not been convinced of his equal citizenship [*gleykhe birgershaft*] in the first place speaks to a real victory of the anarchist word.

It is not infrequently that the anarchist word takes the form of an allegorical fairy tale like *Why?* An anthology of tales of this kind might include works by the brothers

---

4. Boris Yelensky, *In sotsyaln shturem: zikhroynes fun der Rusisher Revolutsye* (Bukhgemeynshaft bay der Yidisher natsyonalistisher gezelshaft, 1967), 133–34.

5. Ibid., 134.

Ricardo and Enrique Flores Magón, Voltairine de Cleyre, Han Ryner, Bernard Lazare, and Gustav Landauer, as well as several anonymous authors of Brazilian *contos*. In the Russian-speaking tradition, alongside the pseudo-folkloric genre of the "revolutionary fairy tale" that had developed since the end of the nineteenth century, we could mention also Stenka Zayets's anarchist fairy tale, *How The Peasants Were Left Without Bosses*, which was first published in 1906 and reprinted in 1917 in the same Biblioteka Anarkhista series.[6] Why should so many such authors have been drawn to the form? The ideologies on display in the stories collected by bourgeois authors such as Charles Perrault or the Brothers Grimm rarely seem anti-authoritarian, to say the least; their formulaic nature speaks to the ritual repetitions of feudal life more than to any utopian or revolutionary vision.

And yet they can afford us some opportunities for reimagining. Consider one particularly strong motif in folklore: the way that the third son, the least likely, the youngest, the most simple-minded, the weakest, often—especially in Russian folklore, as some have observed—turns out to be precisely the one who solves the riddle, slays the giant, undertakes the adventure.[7]

---

6. Sten'ka Zayac, *Kak muzhiki ostalis' bez nachal'stva (Skazka)* [How the peasants were left without bosses (A fairy tale)], Izd-vo Mosk. Federacii Anarhistskih Grupp, 1917.

7. See E. M. Meletinskij, "The 'Low' Hero of the Fairy Tale," *The Study of Russian Folklore*, eds. Felix J. Oinas and Stephen Soudakoff (Boston: De Gruyter Mouton, 2019), 235–58.

This "low hero" has something in common with an even older protagonist: the *eiron*, to whom we owe the word "irony." This is the protagonist of the Socratic dialogues: the person who plays dumb, who adopts the posture of logical weakness all the better to show up the weakness and stupidity of the *alazon*, the braggart, the one who presumes to know. Folktales may reify the stock wisdom of a conformist people, but they can also be used as "weapons of the weak," levers with which to topple conventional wisdom.[8] Such is the Gordin Brothers' protagonist, Pochemu; such are his adventures and misadventures.

Who?

The exiled writer A. Vetluginan ("ill-intentioned" witness, in Slavic scholar Leonid Heller's judgment) attributed the authorship of *Why?* solely to Wolf.[9] Nonetheless, Yelensky referred to this story as one of Abba Gordin's works, though it is signed "Br. Gordin"— "*Brother* Gordin," singular. In life, Abba had, in fact, two: his younger brother, Morris, and his older brother, Wolf. Morris was a dedicated, even fanatical, Bolshevik who later became disillusioned and emigrated to the United

---

8. James C. Scott, *Weapons of the Weak: Everyday Forms of Peasant Resistance* (New Haven: Yale University Press, 2008).

9. Heller, "Voyage au pays de l'anarchie," 259.

States, where he became an equally fanatical Protestant evangelist. Wolf, however, became an anarchist at around the same time as Abba, and the two would collaborate on major educational, literary, political, and philosophical enterprises. Was *Why?* one of them?

"We had a sign among ourselves," Abba writes in his memoirs: "my brother used to sign [his work] 'Brothers Gordin,' and I used to sign 'Br. Gordin,' and works that were truly written by both of us used to be signed by 'Br. W. and A. Gordin.'"[10] In short, Yelensky was apparently correct. Only there seem to be, strictly speaking, *no* works of fiction signed "Br. W. and A. Gordin"—only their early pedagogical writings are signed that way. Others point out that Abba and Wolf both intentionally mystified the question of authorship to create this apocryphal persona, the Gordin Brothers, surely their most lasting literary fiction.[11]

Yet collaborate they most certainly did, from roughly 1908 to 1920, with the first three years of the Russian Revolution marking the highest productive intensity of that collaboration. At its extremes, the "intellectual-emotional intimacy" between the brothers verged on

---

10. Abba Gordin, *Draysik Yor in Lite un Poyln: Oytabyagrafye* (Bukhgemaynshaft bay der Yidisher Ratsyonalistisher gezelshaft, 1958), 211.

11. Nikolai Gerasimov, "Khudozhestvennyye miry russkogo anarkhizma nach. XX v. (problema ideala)." Akrateia, February 3, 2022, https://akrateia.info/hudozhestvennye-miry-russkogo-anarhizma-xx.

something incestuous. In 1958, Abba reflects that he and Wolf had enjoyed "a kind of platonic homosexuality," a "cohesive[ness]" that could manifest itself as "longing."[12] Although in some of his bibliographies Abba Gordin attributes *Why?* to himself alone, hardly any of Abba's or Wolf's individual writings fail to bear the trace of the other brother's influence. Even when, as in 1917, the two were divided by the four hundred miles between Petrograd and Moscow, behind one brother's pen, we can always detect the hand of the other.

Another clue as to the origins of the story is to be found in a short note on "The Anarchist Movement" published in the May 1918 issue of *Anarkhiia*, which was dedicated, among other things, to the oratorical talents of Abba Gordin—talents that were also recognized by Wolf, who for his own part, while an excellent writer, was tongue-tied as an orator, according to the testimonies of his listeners. The article relays how the workers "know [Abba Gordin] well for his performances in the 'little alley' near the Donskoy Monastery, where he improvised his utopian fairy tale How a Peasant Got Into the Land of Anarchy last year." It is not very clear what exactly this practice of improvisation was. Was it a retelling of a work already written with additional elements of improvisation? Or was the utopia itself being composed in the course of these improvisations, which represented live communication, consisting of questions

---

12. A. Gordin, *Draysik Yor*, 458.

and answers, with workers of the nearby Bromley plant during the revolutionary conditions of 1917?

One last complication: on the back cover of the Gordin Brothers' book, *Speeches of the Anarchist* (1919), in a list of works "Available from the warehouse of the First Central Sociotechnicum"—the school the brothers founded in Moscow the year prior—there appears, for the price of two rubles and sixty kopecks, *Why: Or, How a Peasant Got Into the Land of Anarchy*. It is listed under the heading "Gordin *Bros.*"

A Dangerous School

Abba and Wolf Gordin grew up in the town of Smorgon', in the vicinity of what is now Vilnius, Lithuania, in what is now Belarus and was then a Polish province of the Russian Empire. Just as the town's national identity changed with each passing army, the brothers' names, too, would change as they migrated from age to age and from land to land. After entering the United States, Abba Lvovich Gordin would go by Meyer Abba Gordine or Abba Meyer Gordin, while Wolf, also known by the Yiddish and Hebrew versions of his name as Velvel and Ze'ev, respectively, would later forsake both Russian and Yiddish to adopt an ultra-modern name in a language of his own invention.

Sons of the famous Rabbi Yehuda Leib Gordin, the Gaon of Łomża, as Abba would later recall in his memoir,

"Velfke was as wild in his whims and tempestuous in his actions as Abke was calm, mild, and settled."[13] Yet even the young Abba would know the terror of beatings administered by impatient teachers in the heder, the Hebrew school.[14] It was not for nothing that the brothers, in their 1913 pamphlet "Our School" would denounce "the child-Gehennas, where young souls are not listened to but punished," proposing instead that "a school in an oppressed nation like the Jews needs to be and must be a joy: without punishment, without beatings, without rigorous discipline … the Jewish school must be free."[15]

Raised as they were in an atmosphere that hovered between the norms of the Jewish Enlightenment, the secular progressivism of the Labor Zionist youth movement Tzeirei-Tzion, and the ecstatic mystery of Hasidism, the Gordin Brothers would nonetheless grow up to become secular, even atheist Jews.[16] And it was on these princi-

---

13. Ibid., 18.

14. Abba Gordin quoted in J. Aleksandroni, ed., *Memorial Book of the Community of Augustow and Region (Augustów, Poland)*, trans. Rabbi Molly Karp et al. (Tel Aviv: JewishGen Press, 1966), 197. Reproduced online by JewishGen, Inc. and the Yizkor Book Project, https://www.jewishgen.org/yizkor/augustow/augustow.html.

15. Abba Gordin and Wolf Gordin, quoted in Abba Gordin, *Zikhroynes un kheshboynes* (Bukhgemaynshaft bay der Yidisher Ratsyonalistisher gezelshaft, 1957), 196–97.

16. It should be noted that before the revolution, the Gordin Brothers "never even had any connection with anarchists, or with any other political elements" and "didn't need it," as Abba

ples that they founded their first school in 1908. The Gordin Brothers' *"heder metukan"* or "reformed" Hebrew school, which they named Ivriya, was dedicated to teaching the ancient tongue without any reference to God or the Torah.[17] Worse still, it was founded on principles half borrowed from the Yasnaya Polyana school of Leo Tolstoy—"that Bakunin of pedagogy," as the brothers called him—and perhaps others half borrowed from the German radical Max Stirner.[18]

From Tolstoy, they inherited the desire to teach

Gordin's friend P. Gdalia writes. As a result, the appearance of the Gordin Brothers with their unusual ideas in Moscow (Abba) and Petrograd (Wolf) came as a complete surprise to other Russian anarchists, and these ideas themselves "were not properly understood in the philosophical world," despite the fact that their influence during the period of revolution and civil war was rather great. (P. Gdalia, *Kemfer un denker* [Fighter and thinker] (Tel Aviv: Ashueḥ, 1963), 103; 107–108) There is no cause to think that we are better positioned today than the Gordin Brothers' listeners and readers of a hundred years ago, and their ideas are no less unusual and difficult to understand now than they were a century ago.

17. Abba Gordin quoted in Abba Gordin and Hanoch Levin, eds., *Smorgonie, District Vilna: Memorial Book and Testimony (Smarhon, Belarus)*, trans. Jerrold Landau and Sara Mages (Tel Aviv: JewishGen Press, 1965), 193. Reproduced online by JewishGen, Inc. and the Yizkor Book Project, https://www.jewishgen.org/yizkor/smorgon/Smorgon.html.

18. Wolf Gordin and Abba Gordin, *Podrazhatel'no-ponimatel'nyy metod' dlya obucheníya gramote* [Imitative-understanding method for teaching literacy] (Vilna, 1909), 7.

without resorting to the very instruments that conventionally define the school: without authority, hierarchy, coercion. "Only by my moral influence," Tolstoy writes, "did I compel the children to answer as I wished them to do."[19] Yet for the Gordin Brothers, Tolstoy's real contribution, the main criterion for the effectiveness of the anarchist word, the measure of the suitability of the pedagogical method, was *fascination* (*zanimatel'nost'*): "Tolstoy's formula ... states that the method of teaching and school discipline are in inverse proportion: the more fascinating the method, the less its discipline and, conversely, the less fascinating the method, the greater its discipline—this formula will be carved on the tablets of the new pedagogy."[20] Fascination is the element that makes any activity (in the classroom or anywhere else) attractive, the element that resonates with the student's passion (whatever it may be), kindles and strengthens it. This element cannot first be discovered theoretically and then applied in practice; it is found only in practice itself, in improvisation, in the nonviolent interaction and interweaving of passions without power and subordination interceding. If the pedagogical method is fascinating, that is, if the method works, then it does not require

---

19. Leo Tolstoy, "Yasnaya Polyana School," *The Novels and Other Works of Lyof N. Tolstoi: The Long Exile and Other Stories*, trans. Nathan H. Dole (New York: C. Scribner's Sons, 1911), 267.

20. W. Gordin and A. Gordin, *Podrazhatel'no-ponimatel'nyy metod' dlya obucheniya gramote*, 6–7.

the use of violence. The use of violence only indicates that the method itself *does not work*.

From Stirner's egoism, they inherited a shrewd sense of child psychology: "In childhood," Stirner observed, "liberation takes the direction of trying to get to the bottom of things, to get at what is 'behind things' ... therefore we like to smash things, like to rummage through hidden corners, pry after what is covered up or out of the way, and try what we can do with everything."[21] All that resists, all that is hidden— "natural powers" no less than "the mysteriously dreaded might of the rod, the father's stern look, etc."—threatens to overwhelm the child and is therefore an enemy to be fought against: "In childhood, one had to overcome the resistance of the *laws of the world*."[22]

Accordingly, there were no laws to resist in the Gordin Brothers' classroom. In Ivriya, according to one witness, recalling it forty years later in Israel, "They sang and danced at school, painted and sculpted, and engaged in all kinds of work and practical thinking [*ma'asi choshev*]. They didn't sit at all on their benches, they ran around all day long and didn't read a book, even for a short while."[23] No wonder the town's pious Jews warned that

21. Max Stirner, *The Ego and Its Own*, ed. David Leopold, trans. Steven T. Byington (Cambridge: Cambridge University Press, 2000), 13.

22. Ibid., 14–15.

23. Gordin and Levin, eds., *Smorgonie, District Vilna*, 223.

the *heder metukan* was actually a *heder mesukan*, a "dangerous school."

From Books to Bodies

"Practical thinking" could almost have been a Gordin Brothers slogan. Their pedagogy was forged in the belief that action and cognition were intrinsically linked, that, in the words of Pierre-Joseph Proudhon, "the idea is born from action."[24] In a booklet issued by their own publishing house, Novaya Pedagogika, they criticized the established methods for teaching language and literacy, insisting that the key to learning was the body in motion. In some of the early writings, it seems as if the fundamental unit of language for the Gordins was the imperative sentence ("David, sit down!"), which demands concrete enactment rather than the abstract understanding entailed in the declarative ("David is sitting down"). But the imperative does not exercise much fascination—what would induce David to sit down if he himself did not want to? There is no imperative, as we will see, in the Land of Anarchy.

And now the most interesting thing: the anarchic inclination is characteristic not only or primarily

---

24. Daniel Colson, *A Little Philosophical Lexicon of Anarchism from Proudhon to Deleuze*, trans. Jesse Cohn (New York: Minor Compositions, 2019), 139.

of words but of bodies. This inclination the Brothers called "muscularism."[25] Here they seem inclined toward Stirner's concept of the embodied I, the egoistic pedagogy in which it is the flesh that plays the role of the insurgent against external imperatives.[26] In their early pedagogical writings, they outline only the approximate contours of their idea: "We say: people learned to walk because they walked; to speak because they spoke; to write and read because they wrote and read." They continue: "No one learned literacy by letters or sounds, like nobody learned to walk by studying mechanics, to speak by studying phonetics, to see by studying optics, to reason by studying logic, etc., etc."[27] Teaching by doing (with

---

25. Brat'ya Gordinii [Wolf Gordin and Abba Gordin], *Sotsiomagiya I sotsiotekhnika, ili Obshcheznakharstvo i obshchestroitel'stvo* [Sociomagic and sociotechnics, or Generalized quackery versus global construction] (Pervyy tsentral'nyy sotsiotekhnikum, 1918), 15.

26. "Nevertheless it is only through the 'flesh' that I can break the tyranny of mind; for it is only when a man hears his flesh along with the rest of him that he hears himself wholly, and it is only when he wholly hears *himself* that he is a hearing or rational being." Stirner, *The Ego and Its Own*, 60. Subsequently, the Gordin Brothers (and especially Wolf) would bring the idea of muscularism to its extreme conclusion in the insurrectionary ontology of pananarchism (pantechnics, paninventionalism), in which the place of "nature" is occupied by the interweaving of insurrectional bodies (not only human bodies but also the bodies of animals, insects, plants, crystals, organs, planets, and so on).

27. W. Gordin and A. Gordin, *Podrazhatel'no-ponimatel'nyy metod' dlya obucheniya gramote*, 36.

and through the flesh) had been the norm in so-called "primitive" societies, they argued; in "modern" societies, however, "little by little, education moves away from life," instead instructing students that the causes of things were to be found in intangible, abstract entities—"atoms, molecules, ether, electrons, these modern devils."[28] The classroom was not for sitting still in, stilling the body so that the mind could think in detachment ("lifting [it]self in thought above [it]self, and above the world around [it]," as Mikhail Bakunin said). It was to be a "social environment," said the Gordins, in which to experiment with verbal actions, a space for thinking through embodied practice.[29]

It is fitting, then, that in *Why?* our protagonist is a thoroughly concrete thinker—at least, as long as he remains within the social environment of semi-feudal Tsarist Russia. Like one of the illiterate Uzbek and Kirghiz peasants interviewed by Alexander Luria a decade later (1930–1931), Pochemu does not think in terms of such abstractions as "the rule of law" or "rights"; he only recognizes that the man called "judge" is distinguished by his fancy buttons. A transcendental Heaven is beyond what he can imagine, much less the mediating

28. Wolf Gordin and Abba Gordin, *Pedagogika molodezhi ili Reproduktina, Ch. 1: Kritika shkoly* [Pedagogy of youth or reproduction. Part 1: Critique of the school] (Moscow, 1919), 13, 17.

29. Bakunin, *Bakunin on Anarchism*, trans. Sam Dolgoff (Montréal: Black Rose Books, 1980), 272; W. Gordin and A. Gordin, *Pedagogika molodezhi ili Reproduktina*, 37.

role of the Church: "Papa," he innocently exclaims, "why isn't God here? I don't see him!" Without the aid of metaphysical concepts like "sovereignty," he cannot understand how one man, the tsar, can cause everyone to be so afraid of him: "Why do they obey the tsar?! Let them not obey and they will all be tsars." If, ultimately, all that he can understand is that he is being beaten, it is because his social environment does not make any sense.

Muscularism suggests something akin to a sort of skeptical pragmatism, what one might call a panexperimentalism: the muscles question everything and only accept athletic decisions that have no force of law but are open to constant re-questioning. In this regard, the nickname of the protagonist in this tale is symptomatic. This nickname of Pochemu, meaning "why" in Russian, is *a question as such*: "Why" is a question of causes, a question *peri archon* (on the first principles) and thus, is the beginning of all other questions. Unlike the fools of other fairy tales, the know-nothings, ignoramuses, and other such figures of the literary tradition, Pochemu is not someone who asks many questions because of his ignorance. Rather, he is *an embodied question*—"the being of the question," as Gilles Deleuze might say.[30] His interrogative existence is not due to ignorance but to pure curiosity (the Russian word for curiosity [*lyubopyt-stvo*] means "thirst for experiment"). By its structure,

---

30. Gilles Deleuze, *Difference and Repetition,* trans. Paul Patton (London: Continuum, 2001), 64–65.

the story itself sows questions into readers' bodies, into their muscles

This is true of how the Gordin Brothers perceived their works and how they used them. For them, their texts were meant for sowing questions into bodies. Abba's practice of oral improvisation testifies to this. And this applies not only to *Why?* but to their other works, perhaps even to all of them. When arrested during the crackdown of April 12, 1918, Abba did not hesitate to agitate among the guards, asking them the question of, why "if it is not you but Lenin who requires our arrest," the man himself didn't come to capture and guard the prisoners—in much the same spirit as our protagonist, Pochemu. Abba also railed against Lenin's "diarrhea of decrees."[31] In 1919, the question that Abba Gordin had posed to the prison guards would be recorded (almost verbatim), as along with a detailed analysis of "decree magic," in one of the Gordin Brothers' most import- ant philosophical works, *Sociomagic and Sociotechnics [Sotsiomagiya i Sotsiotekhnika]*.

You may then guess, dear reader, what the Gordin Brothers would advise us to do with their books, includ- ing the one you now hold in your hands: they should be treated as scores and played out through your own body in the form of questions addressed to the social and nat- ural environments that surround you.

---

31. A. Lukashin, "12-e aprelya (Vpechatleniya)" [April 12 (Impressions)], *Anarkhiia*, no. 43, April 21, 1918, 4.

Against Science

> Arise, too, you slaves of religion and slaves of
> science; arise and destroy the old world, the world
> of prejudice, superstition, and scientism, the
> world of oppression and violence, the world of
> tears and blood, and make a new world …
> —ABBA L. GORDIN AND WOLF L. GORDIN, *DALOY
> ANARKHIYU!*[32]

The coming of the war swept Ivriya away and scattered the
Gordin family to the world's four corners. Abba and Wolf
became itinerant teachers, following streams of refugees
down the Dnieper River on their way to Mogilev and
Ekaterinoslav. Wolf found passage to Petrograd while
Abba searched for a suitable internal passport allow-
ing him to travel to Moscow.[33] It was during these years,
crossing that sea of boiling blood and tears that was the
Revolution, that the brothers refined one of their most
powerful ideas: pananarchism, or "the Union of the Five
Oppressed." This concept of a union of the oppressed
had been in development since the last days of the heder,
when in 1913, they had published a Yiddish play *Der
yung-mentsh oder der finf-bund: a dramatishe shir in 5 akten
[The young person, or the group of five: a dramatic poem in five*

32. A. Gordin and W. Gordin, *Daloy Anarkhiyu!*, 750.

33. Abraham Samuel Stein, *Dyokna'ot [Portraits]* (M. Neu-
man, 1966), 87; A. Gordin, *Draysik yor*, 465–68.

acts]. Extending anarchist anti-authoritarianism from the sphere of workers oppressed by capitalism and individuals oppressed by the State to those of women oppressed by patriarchy, children oppressed by adults, and nationalities oppressed by colonialism in some ways presaged the development, half a century later, of the New Social Movements, if not that of intersectional analysis. But more than merely adding new concerns to the anarchist agenda, with pananarchism, the Gordin Brothers sought to make a definitive break between anarchism and science.

Bakunin had already spoken of a "revolt of life against science," which certainly entailed a rejection of the Marxian science of history, with its purported "laws" of social development. However, Bakunin had hastened to add, the point was "not to destroy science—that would be high treason to humanity—but to remand it to its place."[34] The Gordin Brothers, in contrast, insisted on the destructive moment, on rejecting "science" *as such*. In their view, the natural sciences were a set of schoolbook abstractions divorced from sensuous, concrete practice:

> All the improvements, professions, trades, operations, occupations, etc., taken together, which are the alpha and omega of civilization, the living spirit, the essence, the quintessence of economic life, instead of all this, school gives us the crooked

---

34. Bakunin, *God and the State* (New York: Dover, 1970), 59, 61.

reflection of the crooked mirror of life, the book, religion-science. Instead of a clean, clear, radiant original, it is a frayed, grayish copy. Instead of world interpretation, explanation of the world, instead of the physical and social environment, it gives the student laws, hypotheses, positions, conclusions about them, instead of living life—dead explanations, interpretations of life.[35]

This was a rather unusual position for anarchists to take in what is sometimes called anarchism's "classical" period (1870–1939), during which anarchist newspapers regularly published updates from the scientific world.[36] "Even if one rejects our extreme demand," the brothers wrote, "that science, like religion ... be banished altogether ... then in any case technics, life-teaching, 'practice' must precede science, go ahead of theory."[37]

---

35. A. Gordin and W. Gordin, *Pedagogika molodezhi*, 6.

36. Russian anarchist history, however, recognizes a "post-classical" period that first emerges not in the 1960s as in the West but in the crisis that was the Revolution itself. See Sergei Fedorovich Udartsev, "Klassicheskiy i postklassicheskiy periody evolyutsii teorii anarkhizma v Rossii," *Evolyutsiya Rossiyskogo i Zarubezhnogo Gosudarstva i Prava. K 80-Letiyu Kafedry Istorii Gosudarstva i Prava Ural'skogo Gos. Yuridich. Unta (1936–2016). Sb. Nauch. Trudov*, ed. A.G. Smykalina, vol. III: Evolyutsiya rossiyskogo gosudarstva i prava, ucheniy o rossiyskom gosudarstve i prave v trudakh-pozdravleniyakh kolleg, (Ekaterinburg: Ural. gos. yurid. untet, 2016), 513–14.

37. A. Gordin and W. Gordin, *Pedagogika molodezhi*, 12.

It is not hard to see how the Gordins could associate technics with the kind of "practical thinking" they favored.[38] But how could technics—so often called by the name "applied science"—be opposed to science *as such*? From their perspective, technics represented concrete knowhow without a further "why," without concern for further explanation—a purely experimental, experiential knowledge-in-action.[39] Science went beyond this to seek abstract, universal knowledge of ultimate principles or causes, the kind of "dead explanations" destined to be distilled into textbooks. In this sense, science had merely displaced religion, leaving untouched the religious metaphysics that had situated God as the ultimate source of order, the unmoved mover. The brothers' disdain for scientific knowledge—"atoms, molecules, ether, electrons," and the rest—was matched only by their zeal for technics and their advancement. "The path to non-science," they insisted, "doesn't mean a return to the

---

38. In the context of the Gordin Brothers' work, we translate *tekhniku* as "technics" rather than "technology" (more directly translated by the cognate *tekhnologii*), with the understanding that "technics" encompass not only things, such as machines and devices, but also the contexts and manners in which they are deployed.

39. In this respect, the Gordins' "technics" resemble James C. Scott's concept of *mētis* or "forms of knowledge embedded in local experience" as opposed to "more general, abstract knowledge." James C. Scott, *Seeing Like a State: How Certain Schemes to Improve the Human Condition Have Failed* (New Haven: Yale University Press, 1998), 311–13.

pre-scientific, to barbarism, but taking a step forward to the post-scientific, to Pantechnics."[40]

It is no surprise, then, that the Land of Anarchy into which our peasant stumbles is a technical paradise where hard labor and the scarcity of goods have been replaced by leisure and plenty. The brothers excuse themselves from describing the workings of the machine that Pochemu is taught to "watch," that is, merely to mind, not to operate. This is a utopia of advanced automation, a leisure communism that they will only fully develop in their subsequent novel, this time a work of science fiction, or perhaps "technical fiction," *Anarkhiia v Mechte: Strana Anarkhiia* (Anarchy in a Dream: The Land of Anarchy).[41]

Worlds Turned Upside Down

What might surprise us is the epistemological reversal that we readers undergo along with Pochemu after we have crossed the sea of boiling blood and tears that was the Revolution, which finds us not in a situation of receiving answers but of more shifting and multiplying questions. If earlier Pochemu is the asker of questions

---

40. Brat'ya Gordinii, *Sotsiomagiya i sotsiotekhnika,* 97.

41. Eugene Kuchinov, "Anarchy as Access to Space: Language, Imagination, Technics." Paper presented at the International Science Fiction and Communism Conference, Sofia, May 25-27, 2018, https://www.academia.edu/41807554/Anarchy _as_Access_to_Space_Language_Imagination_Technics_eng_.

who receives ridicule, threats, or beatings in response, then here Pochemu (our "Why") tries to act as an answerer in the role of "Because." In response, however, he only receives new questions and a sparkling laughter that sounds different in kind than the ridicule he'd previously garnered. Pochemu, who had not understood anything about his world, was constantly seeking explanations; however, when the explanations come to him and he becomes the bearer of knowledge, he encounters only misunderstanding on the part of the inhabitants of the Land of Anarchy. This suggests that "understanding" is indistinguishable from justifying the unjust order of things, that understanding as such must be questioned by (pantechnical) laughter. Pochemu must master this laughter, embody it, and bring it back to the unjust world he left.

Arriving in Petrograd and Moscow in 1917, the brothers found themselves among many other such questioners, in a world where all the institutions of everyday life now had "whys" attached. Workers were questioning the Provisional Government; women were questioning old male prerogatives; ethnic minorities across the Russian empire were questioning the untrammeled hegemony of Russians; students were questioning the power of the police as they took to the streets; individualistic artists were questioning proportion, order, realism, reality itself. It was in this atmosphere of giddy uncertainty that the Gordin Brothers first published *Why? Or, How a Peasant Got Into the Land of Anarchy*.

In this period, Russian reality itself shifted week by week, making friends of enemies and enemies of friends. Wolf and Abba Gordin, who had become editors, respectively, of the influential newspapers *Burevestnik* (*The Petrel*, Petrograd) and *Anarkhiia* (Moscow), were enthusiastic about the February 1917 overthrow of the tsar, and both welcomed and participated in the October Revolution (in which Abba was wounded in action while helping to put down a mutiny of army cadets).[42] But they quickly found their relation to the new government strained. "In the face of the danger of the dictatorship of the landowners and the bourgeoisie," they had written in the Petrograd *Svobodnaya Kommuna* (Free Commune) on September 30, 1917, "we temporarily support the dictatorship of the proletariat."[43] On November 11, they wrote in *Burevestnik* that "the Bolshevik Leninist, in essence, is only a terribly unsystematic and Menshevik anarchist."[44] "We shall overthrow them," vowed Wolf just two days later in a speech in Petrograd.[45]

---

42. Abba Gordin, *Zikhroynes un kheshboynes*, 188–189; V. [Wolf] Gordin, "Doklad Tov[arishcha]. [V.] Gordina 4 Dekabrya (1917 G.) V Komissii Po Sozyvu S"yezda Anarkhistov Rossii," *Anarkhisty: Dokumenty i Materialy, 1883–1935 Gg.*, vol. 2 (Rosspen, 1999), 87–88.

43. Dmitri I. Rublev, *Rossiiskii anarkhizm v XX veke* (Moscow: Rodina, 2019), n.p.

44. Ibid.

45. Gennadii Leontevich Sobolev, *Piterskiye rabochiye v bor'be s kontrrevolyutsiyey v 1917–1918 gg* [Petersburg workers in

So it went, as the Bolshevik government and its left-wing rivals tested their respective strengths. And then came the crackdown: On April 12, 1918, half a year into the revolutionary era, the government's Extraordinary Committee, alleging that anarchists were engaging in criminal activities, launched massive, coordinated raids on the anarchist strongholds. *Anarkhiia* was violently evicted from its premises. Within weeks, *Burevestnik* was shut down as well. After this, the Gordin Brothers came to recognize that the movement was too weak to stand against the regime. For the next six years, they would turn to other strategies of resistance and evasion: to the weapons of the weak.

What you have in your hands is perhaps also a weapon of the weak, a technical object repurposing weakness (economic and logical) as a means to overcome (economic and logical) oppression. Use it wisely.

---

the struggle against counterrevolution in 1917–1918] (Nauka, 1986), 144.

Why?
or, How a Peasant Got Into the Land of Anarchy
(1918)

Today, I will tell you a fairy tale.

Many will say:

"A ridiculous tale."

Some will say:

"A clever tale."

And some:

"This is not a fairy tale but an allegory."

So be it. Let everyone understand the fairy tale in their own way, according to their own understanding. And I will tell it.

I.

There once was a peasant.

"In which country? In which land?"

I do not know.

I only know that he lived.

He was a poor peasant.

And he had four children. I did not know all four well, but I knew the youngest.

"What was his name?"

I know, but I won't tell. Anyway, no one called him by name but by his nickname.

And he had a wonderful nickname.

But I'll tell you about the nickname after.

When he, the youngest, was five years old, they gave him a stick and said:

"Go herd the geese."

And he went to herd the geese.

Sometimes, while he sat alone on a hill, the geese would graze by themselves, and he had nothing to do.

He amused himself with the stick, smacked it on the ground, shouted.

Bored, he laid back. Looked up at the sky.

A summer day. The sun was shining. The sky was clear, immense. And he laid on his back, looking at the sky. So deep. So high. And all there—look—the silken clouds were drifting, drifting, stretching there, there.

And the clouds, like the geese, were white, so white.

Who was grazing there on the blue meadow of the sky?

He watched the clouds.

And there the birds flew. He watched a bird, which quickly, quickly flew away, following it with his eyes until it disappeared.

There it turned black, becoming a dot, hardly there at all.

It was—and was not. Vanished into the sky.

As he was lying and looking at the sky like that, he suddenly heard footsteps and talk.

He rose. Saw children coming. Two boys, followed by a girl.

The boys were so strangely dressed, so strangely dressed. White pants. White sandals. White shirts. White caps.

And they were both so white and clean. And after them, the girl, too, came all in white, all in white. They walked and talked.

But they speak differently, in a foreign language, not as he speaks. And he didn't understand.

As the little gooseherd saw them, he started running from the hillock right toward them, right toward them, with a stick in his hand.

He wanted to ask them:

Why didn't they herd geese?

Why did they speak differently?

Why did they go with the girl?

Why were they dressed so oddly?

And he ran headlong toward them.

They, seeing him, apparently became frightened and ran away as fast as they could. Running and screaming: *Maman, maman*.[1] And the girl, too, was frightened, and also screamed in their language.

He didn't understand at all.

He wanted to ask them:

Why?

And here was the family estate of a wealthy, noble landlord.

In the winter, nobody was at the estate.

In the spring, when the birds came back, the landlord also flew home with his wife and children. And in the fall, when the birds flew overseas, to warmer lands, the landlord flew with them.

The landlord lived like a bird of heaven, flying back and flying away again, even though he had no wings.

A first-class carriage flew in, a first-class carriage flew off.

They ran toward the screams. They caught the little gooseherd. And then they pounded him.

He didn't understand at all.

Why beat him? He wanted to ask:

---

1. "Mama" in French, the preferred language of the pre-Revolution Russian bourgeoisie.

Why?

He still did not understand. Though beaten, he did not understand:

Why didn't they herd geese?

Why were they so wonderfully dressed?

He wore a thick, homespun shirt, bare feet and no hat.

He was dragged into the yard and beaten again.

"Here's a scoundrel! Here's a little prick! Here's a hothead!"

Locked him in a stable.

And he lay on the ground. He hurt from his beating. Well, he would live. He cried, cried, and then stopped. He lay quietly but could not stop thinking:

"Why don't they herd geese?"

The sky was darkening. Twilight fell.

It was dark in the stable. The yard grew quiet.

He was scared, but it didn't matter. What was there to be afraid of?

He was tired of tears and beatings.

And he fell asleep.

He woke up in the morning. He saw his father standing there.

"What are you, crazy, scaring a lord's children?"

"Papa, I didn't scare them."

"What have you been doing? Why are you chasing them with a stick?"

"I wanted to ask them:

Why don't they herd geese?"

Father was laughing. It was annoying but still funny. And the little gooseherd did not understand:

"Why are you laughing?"

And he again asked:

"Why don't they herd geese?"

"You're a queer one! Let's go home! But remember, if you scare them again, you'll be in trouble, you little devil!"

Then his father threatened him with a wagging finger and pulled the boy after him.

But the boy didn't let up on the way:

"Why don't they herd geese?"

He came home. His mother and brothers all rushed at him:

"Why the hell did you go frightening the lord's children?"

"But I didn't frighten them."

"Then why did you chase after them like a hunter after game?"

"I wanted to ask why they don't herd geese."

How angry the mother was, how angry the brothers were—yet they all laughed.

But he didn't calm down.

"Why don't they herd geese?"

They laughed still more.

He asked again:

"Why don't they herd geese?"

The older brother was angry and said:

"Well, shut up with your 'whys.'"

And the second brother said:

"That's what we'll call him, Vanka—*Pochemu*! Why!"

And this nickname stuck. Because of the nickname, his real name was completely forgotten. And everyone began to call him Pochemu.

Pochemu, come here!

Pochemu, bring some water!

Pochemu, drive the horses!

Pochemu, lock the gate!

Pochemu! Pochemu! Pochemu! Why! Why! Why!

II.

A year passed. Two years passed. And he herded the geese as before.

There was a holiday, a big holiday. And new pants were sewn for Pochemu, and he wove himself new bast shoes.

His father took him to church.

And the church was three *versts* from their village.[2]

They went silently. Each was busy with his own thoughts. Suddenly, Pochemu saw a big house, domes, crosses. And the crosses shone and burned in the sun. And around the domes, jackdaws circled.

They came up to it.

A large stone house.

Pochemu gasped in consternation and surprise.

"Papa, whose hut is this? Who lives in this hut?"

"God lives in this hut," was the father's reply.

"And why do we live in a small hut while God lives in a big hut? Why isn't he better off sitting in heaven?"

Father was silent.

And the boy continued:

"And I used to think that God was in the sky, herding the clouds like white geese. I kept looking up into the sky, and I kept thinking, 'Maybe I'll see him.' But God never showed up.

"Never, not once!"

His father was silent. Maybe he didn't want to answer. Maybe he didn't know what to answer.

---

2. A *versta* is equivalent to a little more than one kilometer.

They entered the temple of God.

Pochemu was standing next to his father.

He stood and waited.

Now he would see God, who lived in this hut.

"Papa, why isn't God here? I don't see him!"

"Be quiet!" shouted the father. And the elder brother, who was standing right there, nudged him.

Suddenly a sacred person appeared.

A pope, a priest, a pastor, a mullah—he didn't know.

He wasn't dressed like everyone else, and he looked so strange, so strange.

And why did he rush over there to the pulpit?

"Papa, is that God?"

"Be silent! This is the father. This is a clergyman."

"Why is he not dressed like everyone else if he isn't God?"

"Shut up, will you. He's praying."

"And why does only he pray? Is it his God and not ours?"

"Wait, we'll all be praying now."

"And why does he pray in such a strange way that nothing is clear?"

"Shut up!"

Silence.

Five minutes later. Again, Pochemu asked:

"And why isn't God here?"

"God is in heaven."

"I thought that God is in heaven. Papa, let's go to the

courtyard. You can see the sky there. We'll pray there. If you can't see the sky, then God isn't here."

"Be quiet!"

Silence.

Five minutes later, again Pochemu asked:

"Hey, what are you praying for?"

"I want to be rich."

"And whoever prays a lot is rich?"

"The people God gives wealth to are rich."

"And why doesn't he give everyone money? Is he greedy? Does he have too little?"

"Shut up!"

Silence.

Pochemu thought:

"God is in heaven, yet the hut is on his earth. What does he need a hut for when he has such a beautiful sky?" And Pochemu knew the sky. He stared at the sky all day long. He sought God in the sky, looking, searching, but never seeing him. And Pochemu would have liked to see him at least once.

And the sky could be so beautiful. It could be so blue, all such a light blue. And such a great big round sky, stretching far away. And there the clouds floated—they went somewhere, came from somewhere. The clouds must have seen God.

"Why not go to the field, to the forest, to the meadow, to the hillock and pray there? The sky is there, the clouds are there."

Pochemu glanced around.

There, far away, sat such elegant, such wealthy people.

"Papa, why do the rich pray since they are already rich?"

"Shut up!"

"Papa, then do they pray that we will be poor? And when you pray, Papa, do you become rich?"

Father was silent.

Pochemu thought:

"Beggars are sitting there at the entrance. They all pray—yet they are poor.

Why is this?"

III.

Pochemu found out one day that his father was going to the landlord's. He also wanted to go; he wanted to see the courtyard, the estate.

"Papa, I'm going with you."

"Good."

And they went.

The estate was close by. But Pochemu had never been to the house.

And he was afraid to approach the courtyard alone, having been beaten there and kept locked up in the cattle yard in a stable.

They drew near. He saw the road. The road was planted on both sides with tall, tall poplars. And the trees stood as if stretched out, lined up in a row.

"It's beautiful, said Pochemu. Papa, why don't we have such a road?"

His father was silent.

They were getting very close. They saw the gate. They went in. They saw the courtyard. They saw the semicircle of the garden.

Around the lilac bushes, wild roses. The lilac was blooming. Fragrant.

And there below was a tiny brook, silvery in the sun, which noisily, talkatively fled away somewhere, descending, running off as if to mother, to a large river.

In the middle of the courtyard stood a house, a large house, two stories tall.

Behind the house was a garden.

Pochemu exclaimed in surprise.

"What a hut! Who lives in this hut, Papa?"

"The landlord."

"And this hut must be bigger than God's hut. Is the landlord bigger than God?"

"No, he's a man."

"Papa, why don't we have such a hut?"

"We are poor."

"Why are we poor? After all, you pray."

"God did not give me wealth!"

"Why did he give it to the landlord?"

Pochemu saw the garden. A huge one. And there were a lot of beehives.

And there were many flowerbeds. Children ran back and forth there, chasing butterflies. Children's talk was heard, laughter, fun, joy.

"Papa, why don't we have such a garden?"

They passed through the courtyard. Turned to the side, passing into another yard.

"Papa, why didn't we go straight in? There is a beaten path. And there is a door."

"The lords go there."

"Why aren't we lords?"

"Be quiet!"

They stood in the backyard and waited.

Someone was coming. He was dressed differently, not like a peasant.

"Papa, is this the landlord himself?"

"No! This is his clerk."

His father took off his hat and bowed.

"Papa, why do you take off your hat when he doesn't take his off?"

Father poked him with his elbow, glaring angrily at him so that he would shut up.

They, his father and this man, were talking about something.

Pochemu didn't understand any of it. He heard only the words: *rent*, *soil*, *acreage* …

Pochemu stood silent and was trembling all the same: he was afraid, yet everything was incomprehensible.

On the way back, Pochemu asked:

"Papa, what did you talk to him about?"

"I rent land from him."

"Why doesn't he rent land from you?"

"You're a fool! I take his land, cultivate it, plow it, sow, reap, and pay him for every acre."

"Papa, you work, and still you pay him? Why doesn't he pay you?"

"The land is his, the landlord's!"

"And I thought the land was God's. And whose sky is it—is that the landlord's, too?"

Father laughed.

IV.

A lot of water had flowed under the bridge. Many human tears had been shed. Many times the sun had come and gone. Many times the flowers had bloomed and faded—and Pochemu had grown into a strapping young man.

A handsome boy. Light blond hair. Deep blue eyes. And so cheerful. Everything puzzled him—but everything was funny to him as well.

He was known throughout the whole neighborhood. His name was "Cheerful Pochemu."

He was always cheerful, joyful. But suddenly his questions surrounded him, these "whys" surrounded him—and life didn't seem sweet; it became sad, painful to the point of tears.

Why? Why? Why? Questions buzzed like annoying flies around his ears, gnawed at his heart like a worm, hammered on his brain like a woodpecker: knock and knock.

But everything passed. These questions would be carried away like a thundercloud.

And once again, Pochemu was cheerful; once again, he was glad.

And how should he not rejoice!—The sun shone. The sky was clear. The wind blew. The grass grew. The birds twittered. The flowers were fragrant.

Trees blossomed. Streams flowed. He couldn't have asked for anything better. It was all beautiful as could be.

Everything bloomed. Everything withered. The sun rose and set. People were born and people died.

His father died. His older brother got married. The house was small and crowded. Not much cropland. A bad harvest. There wouldn't be enough bread.

"Pochemu, go to the city to earn money. There are mills and factories there. You will find work and live better than us."

So he went to the city. He went to a big, big city.

"What was the name of that city?"

I don't know. I don't care. There are many such cities in the world.

He took a loaf of bread, black bread, and put it in a sack.

He threw the sack over his shoulder and went on his way. He walked for an hour, and then for another. It was evening. He was in a forest. He lay down on the ground. He spent the night there.

He got up the next morning with the sun. He walked on. For three days he went on.

On the fourth day he saw the domes from afar. He realized that the city was near. He had never seen a big city before.

He sped up his footsteps, curious to see what the big city was like. He got closer. The city stood on a high place.

And the houses were so tall, so tall. And one clung to the next, which was right on top of the next, which pressed against the next, which huddled close to the next.

"Why are they so crowded together? Is there not enough land in God's world? Why do the houses climb so on top of each other? Why do they cling to each other so tightly? Is there not room enough under the sky?"

Why? Why?

Pochemu came into the city. He saw houses standing like two stone walls, with windows and doors in the walls, and in the middle, between the walls, lay a street.

"Why are there no fields? Why are there no meadows? Why are there no gardens?"

There was no greenery, no grass, no bushes, no trees, as if God had cursed this place. The land here was stone—completely paved. And the sky was also not at all like this in the village.

And what about the people?

These questions surrounded him, and he felt sad and thought:

"I'll go up to anyone and ask him, and he'll tell me. They say all the smart people live here. And who should I ask?"

He saw a tall, fat man standing idly in the street. He was not dressed like everyone else, and he had something long and curved hanging at his side. Strange man.

He had never seen such a man before. He was a policeman. He had a saber hanging at his side. He was on guard duty.

Pochemu walked up to him and said:

"Listen, why don't you have any fields here in town? Why aren't there any meadows to graze horses?"

The policeman did not let him finish and said:

"There's a man in a white hat. Go and ask him."

And he thought to himself:

"There is no tsar in his head.[3] He's a fool. He's a wild man."

And Pochemu went up to the gentleman in the white hat, and said:

"Listen, why aren't there any vegetable gardens here?"

He stared at Pochemu with large eyes full of surprise, turned his back without saying anything—and went away quickly, as if he were afraid that Pochemu might chase him.

Pochemu did not understand anything.

"Why did the man in white run away? I'm not a wolf, am I?"

Pochemu approached the policeman again and asked:

"Why did that man run away?"

The policeman got angry and said:

"Get the hell out of here!"

And hit him on the back. It hurt. And Pochemu left. And as he left, he thought:

"Why are they fighting?

"Why are they afraid of me?"

---

3. A Russian expression for someone who is dim-witted, a dullard, which can also indicate a rampage, running amok.

He went down one street and down another. And all the streets were long. And the houses were all tall, so tall. And there were many people in the street, and everyone was running, rushing, hurrying.

"Why are they all in such a hurry?"

He went on. He saw a tall house, its chimneys so high that they reached to the sky, to God, and the smoke was blowing right into the sky. He stopped. He looked. He saw people standing there. They were all blackened, with high-topped boots and black-and-red shirts. He thought:

"These are really our kind of people. They won't beat me."

Pochemu walked up to them and asked:

"Why are you standing here?"

"We've come to work. It's the afternoon shift," the workers said.

"To work!" rejoiced Pochemu. "I want to work!"

"Good! Come with us!"

The gate opened. They came in. They took him to the office.

Some angry gentleman was sitting there.

"What do you want?" he asked Pochemu.

"I want to work!"

"And what can you do?"

"I can herd pigs!"

Everyone laughed, and the angry one was laughing, too, and his belly was bouncing with laughter.

"I can plow the soil, too," Pochemu went on, unashamed.

General laughter.

"I can weave bast shoes."

Everyone was laughing.

The fat gentleman wrote in a thick book "Laborer," and said to him:

"Go with them! They will give you a shovel, and you will dig there."

And Pochemu went.

They dug until late in the evening. Everyone quit digging and he quit, too. They went and put the shovels back into place.

They went back to the office.

They each got two *grivenniks*, and Pochemu got one because he had only worked half a day.[4]

They passed out of the gate.

"Where shall we go?"

"We're going to dinner. And tomorrow at dawn, back to work again."

And so, they left.

They walked down one street, walked down another. Pochemu was not used to walking on cobblestones, on such hard, rocky terrain. His feet were hurting. He looked around.

He saw: cabbies standing, cabbies with horses and cabbies without horses, carriages, and coachmen on the box. He asked:

---

4. A grivennik was a coin worth ten kopecks.

"Why do they stand there?"

"They are waiting for their passengers."

He saw someone come up to the first coachman in the row, sit down, and be driven away.

"Let's get in and go, too! My feet are sore. It is hard to tread on the stones," Pochemu suggested to his comrades.

And the comrades laughed.

"Why are you laughing? The one over there has left, but there are so many cabbies waiting."

"And you will pay the cabby?"

"And I'll pay him."

"Really, with nothing?!"

"How much money do you have?"

"I have a grivennik ..."

Everyone laughed.

"Why are you laughing?" Pochemu asked his comrades.

"It's not enough!"

"So little?" Pochemu asked, surprised. "I have been working for half a day and have not earned enough to ride for half an hour! Why is it so?

"It can't be!"

"You're so funny," say his comrades.

They kept walking. Pochemu was so hungry. He hadn't eaten anything all day.

"I'm hungry! My teeth haven't had a thing to gnaw on all day long."

"It's still a long way to our quarter, to our tavern."

He looked and saw a beautiful house, all lit up with

light from electric bulbs. There were several trees in front of the house.

Between the trees were tables and chairs. At the tables, people were sitting and eating.

Pochemu looked intently and saw everyone sitting at the tables eating, and one was eating black bread with *prostokvasha*.[5]

He was so excited.

"Come on, guys, this way. There is a table and chairs. There's bread and prostokvasha. I want to eat!"

They laughed.

"What are you laughing at?"

"You're so funny!"

"Why am I funny?"

"You have to pay here, too!"

"I know you have to. It's not for nothing."

"Do you have any money to pay?"

"Yes, I do."

"How much?"

"A grivennik." They laughed.

"It's not much!"

"How can it be not much?! I worked till late at night and didn't earn any money for black bread and prostokvasha?! Why is it so?"

Everyone laughed.

---

5. Prostokvasha is a fermented milk product similar to kefir.

One day his comrades spoke to him.

"We will stop working today."

"But why?" asked Pochemu.

"We want the boss to pay us more," His comrades explained to him.

"Why is it we want to be paid more yet the boss doesn't want to pay us more? How can he not, when we don't have enough?"

Everyone laughed.

"And when we don't work, he will pay us more?" asked Pochemu.

"He will."

"Why doesn't he pay us more now?"

"He doesn't want to."

"And why will he want to after?"

Everybody laughed.

"Let's quit working!"

"If my comrades quit working, I'll do it, too; I won't leave my comrades alone!" said Pochemu. They left.

"Come tomorrow," his comrades said to Pochemu, "and we'll all go for a walk and sing songs."

"All right. I will come. Why not sing and walk, if there is no work!

"Where shall we go for a walk?"

"In the streets. It's called a demonstration."

"It doesn't matter what it's called. And what songs shall we sing?"

"Against the tsar."

"Do we really have a tsar? I've never seen him."

"Neither have we seen him."

"What does he do, the tsar?"

"The tsar does nothing."

"Why is he a tsar?"

"He commands that the people be beaten, and he is the tsar."

"Why don't the people beat *him*?"

"They are afraid."

"Who are they afraid of?"

"The tsar."

"Who's afraid?"

"Everyone is afraid."

"Are they all afraid of one man?"

"Yes, we told you: he beats them."

"Who beats them?"

"The tsar!"

"The tsar himself beats all of them?!"

"No. He commands it, and they are beaten."

"Who does he command?"

"The people."

"And who are they beating?"

"The people."

"And why do the people beat the people?"

"The tsar commands it."

"And why do they obey?"

"They're afraid."

"Who are they afraid of?"

"The tsar!"

"And what does he do to make them fear him?"

"He imprisons them."

"The tsar himself?"

"No! He gives orders."

"To whom?"

"The people."

"He orders the people to imprison the people?"

"Yes!"

"And why do they obey him?"

"They are afraid."

"Of whom?"

"The tsar!"

"But he does nothing by himself, so why are they all afraid of just one man?" "Why are all obeying one?"

The comrades laughed:

"You don't understand anything! It's the government—that's who they are afraid of!"

"And who is the government?"

"You know: people, ministers …"

"Are there many of them?"

"No. There are perhaps two dozen of them."

"So why are all the people afraid of them?"

The comrades laughed:

"You don't understand anything. Come tomorrow!"

"I will come!" Pochemu answered.

The next day, everyone gathered at the factory gates. From there they went for a walk around the city. They walked and sang songs. And then Cossacks came to meet them.

Cossacks are people who sit on horseback and hold a whip in their hands.

When they saw the Cossacks, many were frightened and ran away.

But Pochemu walked calmly and hummed.

Why should he be afraid?! Besides, the man on horseback was also a man, not a beast.

The Cossacks came closer. One of them drove his horse straight at him. Almost trampled him.

And began to lash him and beat him with a whip.[6]

"Why are you running straight at me? Is the road not wide enough for you?" Pochemu shouted at him.

And the Cossack beat him.

"Why are you beating me?"

"Why are you singing songs?"

"What's it to you?"

"Those songs are against the tsar!"

The Cossacks surrounded him and started beating him. And he shouted with all his might:

"What do you care? You are not the tsar!"

They took him, beaten, maimed, bleeding, to the station. And from there to the jail, and from the jail to prison.

---

6. The whip here is a *nagaika*, a special kind of horsewhip carried by Cossacks.

Pochemu sat alone in a solitary confinement cell, wondering why:

"Why did they beat me up?

"Why do they keep me here?"

He thought and thought and reflected and reflected, but he had no idea.

"It doesn't matter to them, they're not the tsar! If anyone's against the tsar, let the tsar himself fight him!

"And what's the tsar for?

"What's the government for?

"The tsar doesn't do anything. And who gives him food?

"He says that the people should be beaten, and the people feed him with bread?!

"It can't be!"

He sat like that all day long and pondered.

"It can't be that the people are so stupid as to maintain the government themselves, so that it beats them up and thrashes them. It cannot be!"

The day of the trial came. He was summoned. They took him into a big room, behind a partition. They escorted him out with sabers drawn.

Pochemu didn't understand anything. He asked them:

"Where are you taking me?"

They say:

"We are taking you to court."

"And who will judge me?"

"You'll see," they sneered.

He went in. He sat down on the bench.

There were people sitting at the table. One tall man was in the middle, and the others were on the sides.

"Is this a court?" wondered Pochemu.

They ordered him to stand up. He stood up.

"What is your name?" the gentleman asked him.

Pochemu was not listening. Pochemu looked at the gentleman and saw that he had such buttons. And they all sat in a row.

Sitting and gleaming. He couldn't stand it. He loudly asked the whole hall:

"Why do you have such buttons?"

Everyone laughed.

That gentleman was a little embarrassed and began to whisper something to the others, who were sitting at his side. And then he said:

"I have buttons because I'm a judge."

"Why am I not a judge, but you are?" Pochemu questioned him.

"Silence!" the one with the drawn saber said in his ear.

"What is your name?" the gentleman with the buttons asked again.

"Why do you want to know? After all, it was I who was in prison, not my name."

Laughter again.

And that gentleman said:

"We must know in order to judge you."

"Why are you judging me if I'm not judging you?" asked Pochemu.

General laughter.

"The tsar has ordered you to be judged."

"And who told the tsar to order that?" asked Pochemu.

"No one tells the tsar. He does not obey anyone."

"Why are you obeying him?"

"I am not a tsar," said that gentleman.

"And if you don't obey, will you become a tsar?"

Everyone was silent. Perplexed.

"Silence," said Pochemu with enthusiasm. "So I knew it! He who does not obey anyone is his own tsar."

That gentleman got up and left the room with everyone else.

Pochemu sat and thought:

"Why do they obey the tsar?! Let them not obey and they will all be tsars. Let them not listen to the ministers and they will all be ministers."

The bell rang. The gentleman returned. Everyone followed him in.

He was saying something. He was reading something. They told Pochemu to leave.

He got up and left. Everyone left. He heard what was being said:

"He has no tsar in his head …"

And Pochemu thought to himself:

"And they don't have a head at all but a big tub in place of a head."

Pochemu went out.

Pochemu thought:

"Where should I go?"

I don't want to stay in this city. This city is more tiresome than a bitter radish. There are no fields, no meadows, no vegetable gardens, no grass, no flowers, but there is the tsar, the government, the minister, the policeman, and the Cossacks.

"Why is this so? It would be better if there were no tsar, no government, no policemen, and there were fields, meadows, vegetable gardens, flowers. It's boring here, dusty here, stuffy here. All is stone. The houses are made of stone, the sidewalks are made of stone, the ministers are made of stone, the laws are made of stone, the hearts are made of stone—and you won't find our brother, a peasant, here in the city.

"And where are my comrades?—I don't know.

"I don't know where to find them either."

"I won't stay here anymore," he decided at last. "It's better in our village. There's no tsar, no government, no Cossacks, no ministers, no prisons. You can go for walks there. You can sing as many songs as you like. But you can't do that either here. I'm getting out of here!

"I'm going to look for another place, a better place!"

No sooner said than done: he left.

A day. Two. Three. Four. Five. Six days passed.

At night he slept in the woods. On the way, he picked berries and drank water from streams.

On the seventh day, he saw from afar a terrible sight.

65

Stones were flying up like the birds of the sky. Black rocks.

He came nearer. He saw a river. A great, huge river.

You couldn't see the other side, no matter how hard you looked. And all of it was boiling, bubbling, roaring, churning.

It was raging. It was foaming. It was angry. It was furious. It never rested.

The waves looked like mountains. They first crashed into the sky, then they fell into the abyss and rose up again with such terrible power that they hurled huge rocks out of the depths as if they were the lightest of splinters. And the rocks flew straight up to the clouds, then crashed again into the water. And the water only grew more furious, more boiling, and hurled them up again with such anger, such a roar, that all around the earth trembled and the air groaned. One could go deaf here. Such waves. And there was no wind. No thunderstorm. The water itself was raging, boiling. It could not calm down, could not settle down.

Pochemu listened to the roar of the waves and it seemed he could hear:

The crying of a child. The sobbing of a mother. The moan of a dying man. The sigh of a sick man. The rumble of wheels. The clanking of chains. The ringing of bells.

The beat of a hammer. A terrible explosion. And over it all, a quiet, barely audible weeping.

Pochemu gazed into the waves and saw:

Not water but tears, or blood, warm, red blood …

Why is it boiling?

Why so many tears?

A sea of blood and tears.

Pochemu stood there and thought. He stood for a day, two, three, four, five, six days. On the morning of the seventh day, he looked:

No tears, no blood. All was gone, like a dream, like a vision.

What was the matter with him?

A silent, clear river flowing, winding like a serpent, as if it wanted to take its tail in its mouth and bask in its low, green shores like a child in a cradle.

Without thinking too much, he took off his boots and waded in. He walked.

He saw a mountain. He climbed a mountain. He saw houses in the distance.

He went that way.

Pochemu looked around. He marveled at what he saw: the house stood so tall and beautiful, and around the house there was a garden, a field, a meadow.

And the garden was without a fence. And behind that house, far away, there was another house. Around the house, again, a garden. And that garden, too, was without a fence, not enclosed at all.

And the garden was an orchard.

Was this a city? No, this was not a city, there were no fields or orchards in the city. Here were fields, there were rye and oats, and over there were cabbages and beans.

Was it a village? No, this was not a village. There were no such houses in the village, no big, beautiful houses like these.

He wanted to ask. But whom should he ask? A policeman.

So he went looking for the policeman. He went and looked for one, but he couldn't find one.

They were gone, as if their whole species had died out. He walked down one street, walked down another. And the streets were so wide, so beautiful. Flowers and trees grew on both sides, trees and flowers. There were flowers, but the policeman was gone, as if the earth had swallowed him up.

He thought: "What is this?"

The city was not a city, the village was not a village, but there were no policemen—and even without them PEOPLE lived on.

Finally, he made up his mind. He approached the first man he saw and asked:

"Listen, where's the policeman here?"

"What?" the man said, perplexed. "What do you want?"

"I'm looking for a policeman."

"What's a *po-li-ceman*?" The man could hardly get the word out.

"It's a man who stands in the street and doesn't do anything, but ..."

"We don't have people who don't do anything."

"No. A policeman does things, too. He makes sure people don't walk on the streets."

"We don't have people like that. And why would he watch that they do not walk on the streets?" He shrugged his shoulders.

"Why would he do that? Because they walk against the government, against the bosses."

"We don't have people like that. And what is the government?"

"The government is people who are in charge."

"We don't have people like that. Everyone works here, and no one is in charge."

"What's the name of your city?"

"What is a city?"

"You don't know?! There are cities and there are villages."

"What's a village?"

"What, you don't know?! A village is where the

peasants live, the ordinary men who make bread, and a city is where those who eat bread live."

"We don't have them. Everybody works here, and everybody eats bread."

"Well, I don't know. But what's the name of it all? Pochemu points his hand at houses, orchards, vegetable gardens, and passersby."

"You ask what this country is called? It is called Anarchy."

"What is this street called?"

"Equality."

"And this one?"

"Brotherhood."

"And this one?" Pochemu points to a fourth cross street.

"Freedom."

"And this?"

"Happiness."

"Strange names," said Pochemu.

"Why strange? It's not at all strange. We have all the streets named: Equality, Brotherhood, Freedom and Happiness, and then the following streets of the next quarter: Equality of the 1st, 2nd, 3rd, 4th, 5th, etc."

"And why do you have no policemen?"

"And what are they for us, these policemen?"

"I told you."

"But I didn't understand anything. Tell me sensibly."

"A policeman is a person who impounds [*sazhayet*] another person into prison."

"I don't understand anything. What is being put into the ground [*sazhayut*]? Cabbage?! Where is it being planted? 'In prison'? What is this 'prison'—a garden or what?!"

"No! Prison is a kind of house …"

"I do not understand anything. And I have no time. I'm going to the garden to sing. Today is my day. A lot of people have gathered there. Someone is waiting for me. If you want, come with me!"

"Will they let you?"

"'Let' me how?"

"Will they let you sing in the garden?"

"But who should 'let' me go there?"

"You mean they let everyone in?"

"What do you mean, 'everyone'? Whoever wants to sing, whoever loves and respects singing, comes, and whoever does not love and appreciate it, of course, does not go there."

"So you don't need a ticket," Pochemu tried to explain.

"What 'ticket'?"

"You don't know what a ticket is?"

"I am busy. I'm leaving. Do you want …?"

"I would go, but I want to eat."

"Do you want food? Go to the first dining room you find, and eat there."

"The first?! Everything will probably be expensive there."

"How so, 'expensive'? What is 'expensive'? I don't understand anything you're saying. I'm busy. Goodbye!"

Pochemu stood and thought: "Everything is different here. It's not like in our city. Here everything is so strange.

"Is it really this land, this city that I was looking for in my thoughts, sitting in prison or digging up the earth with a shovel in that big city cursed by God and men alike?"

He was hungry. He was starving. His eyes searched for a tavern, similar to those taverns in which he usually had lunch in that city. He looked in every direction.

"Well, you probably won't find such places here. We must go there, far, to the outskirts of the city. And the city here is so sprawling, so scattered; gardens and vegetable gardens separate one house from the next here so that you can't get to the outskirts in a day." So thought Pochemu, and he became sad.

"It would not hurt to ask for directions and where the nearest inn might be."

He approached the first comer, asking:

"Where is the inn? Or is there a dining room nearby?"

"Yes, right here." The stranger pointed his hand toward a large, tall house. Around the house was a garden. Under the trees were tables. In the middle of the garden, an orchestra was playing.

And at the tables people sat and ate.

Pochemu remained motionless.

"Well, I've showed you."

"Here? … And they'll let me go in there?"

"They'll 'let' you go, somehow?! And who should 'let' you do that?!"

"Well … I have no idea. And how much will you have to pay?"

"What? To 'pay'? How so, to 'pay'? What does it mean to 'pay'?!"

"I don't know. How much money should be given, I think."

"What is 'money,' God be with you?! What are you talking about?"

The stranger thought for a moment, wrinkled his forehead, frowned. Then he brightened up, a smile played on his lips, and he said:

"Oh, it seems you're not from our land. You are from one of those countries. You came to us from there … Where the savage people live?! Isn't that right? How glad I am that one of them has come to us. I've read a lot about them, those savages, in our books. There is much that I did not understand.

"They have some tsars, some republics, some governments. Such funny, hilarious things that you might die laughing."

"You must eat," the stranger changed his tone, "and then I'll go with you to our scientists; they will talk to you, it will be interesting to them, and they will write us books about the savages. Our scientists have written many funny books about you savages. We read these books and laugh so much.

"You've got such a hilarious way of life there that we

can't stop laughing 'til we're on the floor. Go have your lunch, and I'll wait here for you."

Pochemu went up. He saw the gate wide open. In he went.

So he went over to the table and sat down. He sat, but he was still afraid. He looks around, frightened, distrustful; probably the watchman will come and kick him out. He saw people coming in, sitting down at the table. They pressed a button, and a man dressed in white came up to them and asked what they wanted.

They answered him: 1, 2, 3. He walked away. And it all came to the table by itself. Pochemu thought: It's a good idea for me to press this button. So, he pressed it. A man in white came up to him and asked what he would like to eat. He didn't know what to say. He thought:

"I'll ask for a lot; I haven't eaten in days. And tomorrow I might not have anything to eat either. So I'm going to eat for a few days today."

So he said:

"1, 2, 3, 4, 5, 6, 7, 8, 9, 10."

The man in white walked away and laughed a little.

And there were ten dishes on the table. The whole table was filled with them.

Pochemu ate the first course, ate the second, finally, he ate the third. Couldn't eat any more. No more room. He was stuffed. And everyone was looking at him. Why did he have to ask for so many dishes?

Pochemu got up from the table and tried to make his way to the exit.

He walked cautiously, barely moving, as if sneaking; it seemed to him that he was about to be captured, to be overtaken and asked:

"Why, you rascal, you have not paid. Hey, policeman, get him!"

But, thank God, he was already at the gate. There was music playing. He couldn't hear a thing. He kept thinking how the people were all so fine but still very strange. Very different, very foreign.

And that stranger was waiting for him.

"Well, have you eaten?"

"Yes, Pochemu answered."

"Let's go to our scientists. We have two great scholars: one old and one young, both specialists in all that the savage peoples do."

"Let's go."

They passed one street, turned right and then left, then left again.

Pochemu was lagging behind. His feet were aching. He had walked and wandered so much until he got to this wonderful city. Pochemu slowed his pace noticeably. The stranger asked him:

"Are you tired?"

"Yes, I'm tired. I'm exhausted."

"Then come on, let's take a cab!"

"I don't have any money."

"What do you need money for all of a sudden? We don't have money."

"Seriously, you don't have money?" The stranger

called for a driver. He pulled up. Both sat down and continued the interrupted conversation.

"You really don't have money?

"You're poor?"

"What is 'poor'?"

"Poor is the one who is not rich."

"And what is 'rich'? I do not understand what you say."

"The one who has a lot of money is rich."

"Well, we don't have money."

"How can you not have money?"

"It's simple: no one has it. No one in our whole country has it."

"How can that be?" Pochemu raised his hands in amazement.

"Look around you!"

"Yes, I'm looking! Here we are, riding in a cab. Where I came from, only the rich ride in cabs, and who's going to pay him?"

"Pay who?"

"The cabby who is driving us."

"Nobody."

"Then what does he live on?"

"What do you mean, what does he live on?"

"What does he do for a living? What does he live on?" Pochemu was perplexed.

"What does he live on?" The stranger looked even more puzzled. "He was born into God's world and lives until he dies. And we live long lives here."

77

"I don't understand, what does he live on? Where does he get his food?"

"Where?! He eats in the canteen."

"And what does he pay there?"

"You ate there yourself: no one pays."

"What do you mean no one pays? They never pay? I thought it was just a case of 'Today you can finish your meal for free, but tomorrow you can't.'"

"Well, to eat—I already know, he eats there. But where does he get his clothes?"

"Where? Where does he get them from? He takes them from the warehouse."

"Where does the warehouse get them?"

"What do you mean 'where does the warehouse get them'? We work, we sew, we take the clothing to the warehouse. Everyone goes there and takes what they need."

"What do they pay you for your work?"

"What do you mean, 'pay'? And who should pay? We all work. Everything is ours."

"And you don't get paid?"

"Of course, we don't get paid. And we don't pay anything."

"How much do you get for your work?"

"How much do we get?! We get nothing."

"Why do you have to work?"

"Why do we have to work?! What do you mean, we 'have to' work? We all work. It's boring without work. Everyone here works. Only the sick don't work and the little kids, the little ones who play and fool around."

"It is strange here. It's good here but strange; I don't understand it."

"Here, we must get down. Here are our scientists."

Pochemu saw a great, beautiful house, all covered with greenery and flowers.

"Is this their house?" asked Pochemu.

"What do you mean 'their' house?!" the stranger replied, not understanding.

"I asked if this house belongs to the scientists. Is it their home or not?"

"I do not understand you at all; what does it mean, the house 'belongs' to them?"

"How do you not understand? It is theirs, they live in it."

"How do they 'live' in the house? They are born and live, but what does the house have to do with it?!"

"Well, what do they do here?"

"They sit here, write books, read, and listen to talks."

"Whose house is it?" persists Pochemu.

"Whose house? It's like all houses. Whose house could it be?"

"I don't understand." Pochemu finally gave up.

"Let's go."

They went in.

They passed through the first hall, and Pochemu saw that everyone was sitting and reading.

When they passed through the second hall, he saw

that everyone was sitting and writing. When they passed through the third, he saw that everyone was sitting and listening, and one old man was standing on a dais and speaking. And all around him sat and listened.

At times they wrote in their books. At times they laughed.

The stranger he came with pointed him to a bench and said:

"Here, sit down."

He sat down on the bench in front of a small round table. The stranger sat down next to him ...

He sat and listened. The hall was silent and quiet. Only the old man's voice could be heard:

"There are several other savage nations in the world. They live in Europe. Their morals are harsh. They are angry, vengeful, and proud. They consider themselves 'cultured nations.' And they have tsars, presidents, states, republics, permanent and provisional governments."

"What is a tsar?" The students asked.

"A tsar," the old man replied, "is a man who is sillier than everyone else but thinks he is smarter and better than everyone else, so he commands everyone."

"And what is a president?" the listeners asked again.

"The president," answered the old man, "is the same as a tsar but an elected tsar, and they elect him for three years or for seven years, so that he commands them.

"And why do they elect him to command them?"

"Of course, they don't need him; that's why they are savages, for they elect people they don't need."

"And what is a government?" the listeners went on to ask.

"A government is a few men whom the tsar elects, or whom a small part of the people elects, who don't do anything but again and again order whatever they please, whatever pops into their 'government heads,' and everyone must listen to them without question and obey them."

"And of what use is this government to them?" The listeners were perplexed.

"Of course, they don't need it. The government needs the people. It cannot exist without the people, for if the people do not give them food to eat, they, all the rulers, will starve to death. And the people need the government like a healthy leg needs a crutch."

"So, what do they elect them for?"

"For the same reason that they are savages. Either they are savages because they elect them, or they elect them because they are savages," said the teacher, laughing.

General laughter.

The stranger stood up.

The old man asked him:

"What did you want to say?"

"I wanted to tell you that one from those savage nations has come to us."

"Really? From one of those nations? That's interesting. Bring him here quickly, and let him tell us about their savage way of life," said the old man, pleased and excited.

"Here he is. In the hall."

"Where?" was the general question.

"There he sits."

The old man stepped down from the pulpit. Walked up to Pochemu. Addressed him:

"Are you from one of those savage countries?"

"I don't know. Our people say they are not savages."

"They are savage nations. What they say doesn't mean anything. And a crazy man never knows he's crazy."

Everybody laughed. Pochemu laughed, too.

Old man: "What's your name?"

"My name is Pochemu!"

Old man: "Why is your name Pochemu?"

"I don't know why, maybe because I kept asking 'why?' I didn't like a lot of things about us, and I kept asking why it was so and not otherwise."

The old man took out a big book and wrote:

"Among the savage nations, whoever asks questions and wants things to be different, they call him Pochemu—'Why.'"

"Well, tell us about life there, their way of life, their wild, harsh mores, and their turmoil."

"Where should I start?"

"What city are you from?"

"Our town was called Falsehood."

The old man went to the wall. On the wall hung a huge convex map, painted in different colors. He searched and searched, then pointed with his finger, and said:

"That's where he's from."

Listeners surrounded him. He explained:

"See, over there in the black live those savage tribes

that have tsars. You see the blue, there live those savage peoples who have republics. And over there you see the pinkish color, there live those savages who have democratic republics. And over there you see the red, there live those savages who have provisional governments, revolutionary governments."

"Well, Pochemu, explain it to us!" everyone began to ask him.

"I don't know where to start," was his answer.

"What do you mean you don't know?" The old man said, "Whatever you tell us, all of it will be interesting. I've read a lot of books about them, about those savages, and I've written a lot myself, but I've never been there. I'm afraid to go there, to the savages."

"Afraid of what?"

"The books say they are all robbers, all murderers. And whoever murders 100,000 people is called a hero and then becomes a tsar. They even erect monuments to these murderers."

"No. We don't only have murderers; we also have thieves."

"I know what murderers are, I've read about them. They are called soldiers, officers, generals, commanders-in-chief, military ministers.

That I know. But what are 'thieves'?"

"What are 'thieves'?"

"Explain this word to us. We don't understand it. We know that in your country, they teach the murderer for three years how to be a murderer. And everyone is obligated to be one; you have military conscription, i.e., 'bandit duty.' But what thieves are, that we don't know."

"How can you not know! A thief is someone who comes in at night, picks a lock, and steals whatever he finds."

"I don't understand any of that."

"What don't you understand?!"

"I'm telling you, I don't understand anything. You say a thief comes in at night and breaks the lock and steals. What's a 'thief'? What's a 'lock'? And what's 'stealing'? I don't understand anything. You speak incomprehensible words."

"How do you not know what a lock is?"

"Of course I don't."

"A lock is one made of iron, and it's curved on top, and they lock the door at night with it."

"I don't know what a lock is. Draw for me: here's a pencil."

"I can't draw. I didn't study how."

"He cannot draw!" shouted all at once in surprise, looking at each other. "Don't they teach everyone at your school?"

"No."

The scientist wrote in his book:

"Savages don't teach in schools."

"Are there schools?"

"There are."

"And who goes there?"

"Only the rich."

Everyone gasped in astonishment.

"Strange people, savage people! People don't go to school!"

"And what is a 'lock'? I still do not understand."

"You lock a door at night."

"Why lock it?"

"Why, so the thieves don't come."

"Why not let them come?"

"If you let them come, they'll take away everything."

"Let them take it all away. Why should they take it?! It's useless work."

"Let them take it?! It's mine, and he comes and takes it."

"What do you mean it's yours and he takes it?"

"Well, for example, these are my boots, and he takes them."

"How are they yours? They're boots, that's all. And what does he need them for? Let him go to the warehouse and take them for himself."

"Well, for instance, this is my house …"

"How is this your house? I understand: your son, your daughter, your father, your mother. But how could he take them for himself? And the house, how can it be yours? Did you give birth to it?"

The learned old man wrote hastily in the book:

"The wild peoples have a belief that they give birth to their houses, and they have them. Everyone has his own house, like we have our own mothers."

"No, not so," interrupts Pochemu. "I did not give birth to it. I bought it."

"How did you buy it?"

"I gave money for it."

"You gave money for it, and then what?"

"Nothing. It's mine."

"What are you doing with it?"

"I don't do anything with it. I live in it."

"How do you live in it?"

"How does a man 'live' in a house?"

"He told me so on the road, too, but I didn't understand anything," the stranger interjected.

The scholar wrote in his book:

"There is a belief among wild peoples that people live in houses like shells, or like a turtle under its shield."

"No, they don't," objected Pochemu. "The one who pays the money buys or rents [*snimayet*] his own apartment."

"How does he take away [*snimayet*]? What does he take away? What do you have to rent to live there?"

"They don't take away anything, they just pay money."

"I don't understand," said the scientist in despair. "You should explain to us first what a 'thief' is, maybe then I'll understand it, too."

"He who takes for himself. He who comes at night and steals, he is a thief."

"Why should he come at night? Let him come during the day."

"He is afraid in the daytime."

The scholar wrote hastily in his book:

"The savages have people who are afraid to walk in the daytime and only walk at night."

"No, not so. He is not afraid of walking in the daytime, but he is afraid of stealing in the daytime. They will see him and put him in jail."

"Who will put him there?"

"The policeman will lock him up."

"What is a 'policeman'?" asked the old scholar, annoyed to see that he would understand nothing here. "These savages are too savage for a man who is not a savage to understand them," he thought to himself.

"A policeman is a man who puts thieves in jail, while he himself stands in the street, on guard," said Pochemu persuasively, proudly, knowing that he knew so much and that the scholar knew nothing.

The scientist took up the book with annoyance and wrote:

"The savages have two kinds of people: one kind stands in the street and puts other people in prisons; the other kind sits in prisons."

"No, not so!" said Pochemu impatiently. "The policeman is an officer of the law, a guardian, a watchman."

"I don't know what that is," said the scholar, grinning. "We have no such men. But tell me, is a policeman above the president or below? Or a minister, or above the rank of a minister?"

"It's the same thing," said Pochemu at last, though he knew it wasn't exactly, but he felt awkward not being able to explain what a policeman was.

The scholar wrote with satisfaction:

"Among savages, the policemen are called ministers and some ministers are called policemen."

"That's not quite true," Pochemu said, hesitating.

But the scholar became stubborn:

"How it is not so?! That's what it is! You can say: 'Mister Minister,' or you can say: 'Mister Policeman.' I know. I have read many books about those savages," the old scholar backed up his words with a gesture toward the books he had read.

Pochemu didn't have the courage to argue, and to get out of the situation he added:

"A policeman is a little minister; a minister is a big policeman."

"That's what I wrote," said the scholar in a triumphant tone. "Now, explain to me what a 'thief' is. We have none of those, and we cannot understand it."

"I told you: a thief is someone who takes my ..."

"Where did you get yours? You took it, too, and you're a thief, too. So, everyone is a thief."

The scientist was delighted with his discovery and wrote in his book:

"Among the savages, all people are thieves. You can just call them savages, and you can call them, in their own way, thieves."

"No, it is not so," argued Pochemu. "I bought and took, but he steals."

"And what is 'stealing'?" Again the old scientist did not understand.

"Stealing is taking at night, when no one is looking."

The scholar rejoiced, and with a bright smile on his lips and in his eyes, he wrote in the book:

"Among those savage peoples there are those who buy, they take by day, and there are those who steal, they take by night."

"No, not like that," Pochemu nearly got angry at the old scholar's lack of comprehension. "If they buy, they are not thieves."

"And if they buy, then don't they have to take?" asked the puzzled scientist.

"They have to," answered Pochemu coolly and confusedly, feeling that the scientist was getting the best of him.

"I'll write it this way:"

"With savages, all men are thieves, but there are thieves who buy and steal, and there are men who do not buy but take and steal."

"No! It's not like that!" Pochemu, feeling a burst of excitement, insisted again. "When you buy and take, you are not a thief. That's how it's understood with us. It's the law," he added, feeling the weakness of the argument. "And if you don't buy and take, it is against the law, and you are a thief."

"I shall write so," said the scholar in a firm and resolute voice. "I will write:

"There are thieves who steal by law, and there are thieves who steal without law."

"Let it be so," Pochemu at last surrendered.

"Now, explain to me, what is a 'lock'?" said the scientist in a soft, pleading voice.

"A lock hangs on the door. Everything is locked up. Even the little children among us know what a lock is."

"What," asked the scientist, "do you have little children locked up, too?"

"No. They lock the door so that no one can open it."

"Why would you lock it so that no one can open it?"

"Why? So no one can break in!"

"So no one can break in where?"

"Why would they break in when they can get in through the door?"

"No. The door is locked."

"That's what I'll write." He wrote:

"The savages lock the doors and climb in through the windows."

"No, not all of us. Only thieves."

"You're at it again with the thieves. I don't understand it again," said the scientist angrily. "You're tired today, that's why you can't explain things properly. Go and rest and come back tomorrow. You tell me all about it, and I'll write it all down in the book. We think it's very funny how you lock the doors."

Pochemu said goodbye and went out with the stranger he came in with.

"I'm hungry," said Pochemu.

"Let's go to dinner. It's about time."

"Where shall we eat?"

"Here we are."

"They went into the tearoom."

And the tearoom was all glass and mirrors, and the ceiling and the floor and all four walls. And there was a garden around the teahouse. It was getting dark.

The lanterns were lit. And the lanterns were hidden between the leaves, their light falling as if the moon were peeking out. So beautiful, so beautiful. Then music was playing. The singer sang:

> "All the people are like brothers,
>   You are welcomed
>   Everywhere and everywhere with hugs
>   And brotherly embrace."

"Yes," thought Pochemu, "here people are like brothers. All for one. One for all. All for everyone. All for all."

They sat down at a table. A meal was served to them. Pochemu ate, slowly.

He kept thinking: "How nice it is here!"

Music was playing. A singer was singing. There was a deep silence all around, everyone listening to the great singer. And Pochemu listened.

What simple words, but how much truth in them.

"Here people are brothers! My own brothers!" He whispered, not feeling it himself.

They finished their supper. They went out. It was bright outside, charmingly bright.

There was a quiet, pleasant light, as if drizzled down

in silver drops. You couldn't see the lanterns hidden between the leaves.

"Maybe you want to rest?" the stranger asked Pochemu.

"Yes, I do. I'm so tired. I've seen so many new things at once, in one day. I'm tired."

"Come. I'll take you."

"Where to? To a bunkhouse?"

"To either the 'Goodnight' or the 'Pleasant Sleep' Sleephouses."

"Where are they?"

"They're right across the street."

"How much do you pay for a night's lodging?"

"Shame on you. How many times have you been told that we don't pay here, and you keep saying: 'How much do you pay?'"

"I forgot. Everything is so unfamiliar. Everything is so good."

"Let's go."

They crossed to the other side. They entered a big, dense garden.

In the middle of the garden there was a house. They entered the house. The house was divided by corridors.

There were rooms on both sides of the corridor. Above each room was a number 1, 2, 3, etc., and a note, "Occupied" or "Vacant."

"See, here's a vacant room. You can sleep here. Tomorrow morning I'll come by your place. We'll have breakfast and go back to that scientist. You're a treasure for us. In the meantime, goodbye."

"Wait. Don't go away. Maybe there's something I won't know. How to lie down, how to light a fire, how to put it out. Come in, teach me."

"Let's go in."

In they went. It was a nice, clean, quadrangular room with two windows. The windows faced the garden. A door stood between the windows, leading out into the garden.

In the middle of the room was a bed.

Pochemu walked over to the bed, looked at the pillows.

"So white as snow, like those geese I used to herd."

He felt the pillows.

"How soft they are!"

"They are made of sea grass.

And you see, this is how you light a nightlight. And this is how you put out the fire." He showed him.

"I was about to leave. And here's a little library for bedtime reading. A gramophone reads them. It recites fairy tales or sings children's songs."

"And what's that?" asked Pochemu, pointing to the clothes that hung on the wall and the shoes that stood against the wall.

"These are for you. Tomorrow you will dress our way."

"Good night!"

"Good night!"

The stranger went out. Pochemu undressed. He had never slept in such a bed in his life. All clean and white, like a silken summer cloud.

"And what is this shirt for?"

He wondered what the nightwear was for.

He undressed and lay down. But for a long time he could not sleep.

"Everything is different here. It's not the same as over there. It's a good thing that he escaped. There are savages there. Everyone should escape that place. All of them. No one should stay there. Only animals will live there, and people will all come and live here."

The windows were open. He got up, went to the window and was about to lock it for fear that someone would break in.

But suddenly he remembered that no one here even knew what a thief was. No matter how much they were told they did not understand it. He went and lay down again.

Five minutes later, he forgot again. He jumped out of bed and went to the door and wanted to lock it. Tried it this way and that, but it wouldn't lock. He looked: there was no lock, no key, no latch, no deadbolt. Suddenly, he remembered where he was. He laughed. Laughing at himself, he said in a half-voice:

"I had forgotten that I have left those savage people, where everyone locks themselves in, where everyone fears their neighbor as their enemy."

He lay down. He fell asleep.

He slept soundly. In Anarchy, they slept quietly, not anxiously but soundly, the sleep of righteous toilers.

He woke up in the morning. The clock struck. He

counted: it had struck nine.

It was late. Everyone here must be up early. He jumped out of bed.

Took a swim in the pool. Washed himself. Put on the new outfit.

He felt a little uncomfortable in his new clothes. There came a knock. He went out to meet them: it was yesterday's stranger knocking.

"Good morning. I did not recognize you in your new clothes. I see another man coming out of this room. How did you sleep?"

"I slept well."

"Are you hungry?"

"No! I just got up."

"Let's go for breakfast, and from there straight to our scientists. They already asked for you on the phone."

"Let's go, but I'm not hungry."

"Let's go."

They ate breakfast and drove to the Temple of Knowledge, to see the scholars.

And there they were already waiting. The room was packed. The audience was fully assembled. Everyone wanted to see him, to hear his stories, his unbelievable and incomprehensible stories about those savage people.

He came in. He said hello. Two scientists came up to him: an old man and a young man, and they spoke to him:

"So, tell us about it."

"I do not know where to begin."

"Tell us about your life: Where did you grow up? Where did you study? How did you study? Where did you work? Tell us everything, in order. And we'll call our book just that: *A Life Story: The Story of a Savage European*." And he began to tell the story. They didn't understand much. He had to explain everything to them. It was hard for them to understand. In particular, they did not understand what a landowner, a lord, a peasant, a factory man, a worker was.

For three whole years he stood there and told his stories, and they wrote them all down, provided explanations, and published them.

And everyone read these books, from old to young, from young to old, from the gray-haired old man to the elementary schoolboy who had just learned to read. And those who could not read themselves, their nannies, teachers, and tutors read to them.

And, reading these books, they laughed. They laughed until they fell over, until they were out of breath.

And in that country of Freedom, they say:

"It's funny, like a story about savage Europeans."

And when they scare the children, they say:

"The minister is coming! The provisional government is coming!"

At the end of three years, Pochemu finished his biography.

And he asked to be given a job.

He was taken to the Temple of Labor. I cannot describe this temple.

It cannot be described in words, nor can it be told of in a fairy tale.

They brought him into a separate room. They taught him to watch the machine. They showed him how and what to do, and then they left. When an hour had passed, his friend came in and said:

"In view of the fact that you work with us for the first time and are unfamiliar with our customs, I announce to you that after the first hour, if you want, you can rest ten minutes; after the second hour, fifteen minutes; and after the third, thirty-five minutes," he said, and left.

They leave for work very early there, at 5 a.m.

When the clock struck ten, the same comrade came in and told him:

"If you want to work more, you can, but it's customary for us to work only four hours. We do not force anyone to work. But usually after ten no one works, and from five to ten everyone works."

"What do you do all day?"

"As anyone likes: one draws, another sings, a third plays an instrument, a fourth writes tales, and a fifth composes songs, and whoever wants to invents machines. All the young men are fond of this. And in the evenings, we all go to theaters, to the philharmonic, to concerts, to recitations."

"*We* have eight hours of work. And the owners shout that it's not enough, that we are idlers," Pochemu said with vexation.

"Is that really true?! Do you really work eight hours? Truly?"

"Truly!"

Pitiful, unhappy people, savages!

He lived in the land of Anarchy for ten years. He remembered his comrades, his brothers, his relatives, and thought:

"I pity them, for they are wasting away there. So, he went to his homeland, his savage homeland."

Now he travels around villages, cities, everywhere that people gather, and tells of how people live in Anarchy. And ending his story, he adds:

"Either we will leave, comrades, for the land of Anarchy, or we will arrange our lives here so that it is here as it is there. After all, it's a shame: we are scolded as savages there."

AK PRESS is small, in terms of staff and resources, but we also manage to be one of the world's most productive anarchist publishing houses. We publish close to twenty books every year, and distribute thousands of other titles published by like-minded independent presses and projects from around the globe. We're entirely worker run and democratically managed. We operate without a corporate structure—no boss, no managers, no bullshit.

The **FRIENDS OF AK PRESS** program is a way you can directly contribute to the continued existence of AK Press, and ensure that we're able to keep publishing books like this one! Friends pay $25 a month directly into our publishing account ($30 for Canada, $35 for international), and receive a copy of every book AK Press publishes for the duration of their membership! Friends also receive a discount on anything they order from our website or buy at a table: 50% on AK titles, and 30% on everything else. We have a Friends of AK ebook program as well: $15 a month gets you an electronic copy of every book we publish for the duration of your membership. *You can even sponsor a very discounted membership for someone in prison.*

Email **friendsofak@akpress.org** for more info, or visit the website: **https://www.akpress.org/friends.html**.

There are always great book projects in the works—so sign up now to become a Friend of AK Press, and let the presses roll!